The
Outlaw FROM
OUTER Space

AN INTERACTIVE MYSTERY ADVENTURE

by Steve Brezenoff
illustrated by Marcos Calo

Field Trip Mysteries Adventures
are published by Stone Arch Books
A Capstone Imprint
1710 Roe Crest Drive
North Mankato, Minnesota 55603
www.mycapstone.com

Library of Congress Cataloging-in-Publication Data is available online
Names: Brezenoff, Steven, author. | Calo, Marcos, illustrator. |
Brezenoff, Steven. Field trip mysteries.
Title: The outlaw from outer space : an interactive mystery adventure /
by Steve Brezenoff ; illustrated by Marcos Calo.
Other titles: You choose books.
Description: North Mankato, Minnesota : Stone Arch Books, a Capstone
imprint, [2017] | Series: You choose stories. Field trip mysteries |
Summary: Sam, Egg, Gum and Cat, and the other members of the Franklin
Middle School Science Club are on a guided tour of Greater River City
Air Force Base (otherwise known as Zone 99) an aspiring science
museum, and Gum is convinced that if they can sneak away from the
group they will find evidence of aliens--and it is up to the reader
to choose how their adventure unfolds.
Identifiers: LCCN 2016038062| ISBN 9781496526441 (library binding) |
ISBN 9781496526489 (pbk.) | ISBN 9781496526526 (ebook (pdf))
Subjects: LCSH: School field trips—Juvenile fiction. |
Extraterrestrial beings—Juvenile fiction. | Science museums—
Juvenile fiction. | Plot-your-own stories. | CYAC: Mystery and
detective stories. | School field trips—Fiction. | Extraterrestrial
beings—Fiction. | Museums—Fiction. | Plot-your-own stories. |
GSAFD: Mystery fiction. | LCGFT: Detective and mystery fiction.
Classification: LCC PZ7.B7576 Ou 2017 | DDC 813.6 [Fic] —dc23
LC record available at https://lccn.loc.gov/2016038062

Graphic Designer: Kristi Carlson
Editor: Megan Atwood
Production Artist: Laura Manthe

Summary: Follow Sam, Egg, Gum, and Cat as they try to solve the mystery
on their field trip to a notoriously mysterious military station, Area 99.
After a few mysterious thefts, some scary claw marks, and more than a
couple of strange noises, the junior detectives need to solve the case:
could it really be an alien?

Printed in Canada.
010050S17

YOU CHOOSE STORIES
A FIELD TRIP MYSTERIES ADVENTURE

The Outlaw FROM OUTER Space

STONE ARCH BOOKS
a capstone imprint

STUDENTS

Catalina Duran

A.K.A.: Cat

BIRTHDAY: February 15t

LEVEL: 6th Grade

INTERESTS:

Animals, being "green

field trips

Edward G. Garrison

A.K.A.: Egg

BIRTHDAY: May 14th

LEVEL: 6th Grade

INTERESTS:

Photography, field trips

James Shoo

A.K.A.: Gum

BIRTHDAY: November 19th

LEVEL: 6th Grade

INTERESTS:

Gum-chewing, field trips, and showing everyone what a crook Anton Gutman is

Samantha Archer

A.K.A.: Sam

BIRTHDAY: August 20th

LEVEL: 6th Grade

INTERESTS:

Old movies, field trips

FIELD TRIP 🚌 MYSTERIES

The Franklin Middle School field trip bus has been rolling along straight, flat roads for over an hour.

"Come on, come on, come on," says James Shoo, better known as Gum. "When are we going to get there?"

"Won't be long now, I think," says his friend Edward Garrison. His friends call him Egg.

Catalina Duran, sitting across the aisle, leans closer to them. "He's right," Cat says, and then adds in a whisper, "I can tell because we're in the middle of nowhere. That's how Zone 99 keeps all its secrets."

Gum's eyes go wide. "Good point," he says. "Out here no one would ever know about their alien experiments!"

TURN THE PAGE.

Egg rolls his eyes. "Cat," he says, "please don't encourage Gum. He really believes we're going to see aliens at an Air Force base!"

"We are," Gum insists. "Who's better at snooping around than we are?"

Cat laughs. "I think it's fun," she says. "Even if it's not true, we can pretend there are aliens."

"Oh, it's true," Gum says.

Next to Cat is their other best friend, Samantha Archer, who smiles.

"Reminds me of some of Grandpa's favorite movies," she says. Sam's parents died when she was a baby, so she lives with her grandparents. "Aliens and spaceships and ray guns. This trip is going to be a hoot and a half."

Suddenly, Gum jumps up and leans over the seat in front of him, pointing wildly out the window. "We're here!"

Up ahead, a huge chain-link gate rolls open. The bus pulls up to the little guardhouse.

A man in a black uniform wearing a black cap steps out of the building and climbs aboard the bus.

"Franklin Middle School Science Club," the man says, pulling off his cap. "Slow day here at the base. We've been expecting you. Pull on in, and park in the lot on the south end of the main building."

The man steps off the bus, then the bus rolls on through. It's a long way to the main building. The parking lot is empty.

"He wasn't kidding about it being a slow day," Egg says as the kids climb off.

The science club has twelve members. It used to be smaller, but a very exciting trip to the zoo started a rush of new members.

Ms. Marlow is the teacher-advisor for the club. Even though the role was supposed to be temporary, she liked it. And since the club members liked her too, she stuck around.

Standing near the bus as the kids climb off is a woman in a pale green shirt and dark brown pants. A green cap sits atop her neat bun of blond hair.

TURN THE PAGE.

"Welcome to the former Greater River City Air Force Base," she says, grinning.

"You mean Zone 99," Gum says.

Egg covers his face with his hands, mortified, while Cat and Sam chuckle.

"Ah, right," the woman says. "I'm Sergeant Houlihan and I'll be your guide this morning. Please follow me." She leads them toward the front entrance.

"Hey," Anton calls from the back. He's not even supposed to be in the science club, but Mr. Neff made him join after he caught Anton goofing off one too many times in science class. "Why can't we just go in there?"

Anton points to a metal door much closer than the entrance.

"That door is for emergencies only," the sergeant says. But then she glances at the door and notices it's ajar.

"Who did this?" she says, hurrying to the door and shoving it closed. "This way, *please*."

The science club and their chaperones follow the sergeant through the front doors, and everyone gasps.

The front lobby is a mess. Chairs are knocked down. Plants are turned over, their soil spilling all over the carpet.

"Was it like this before you came to get us?" Ms. Marlow asks.

"I have no idea!" Sergeant Houlihan says. "I used the employee entrance to come in this morning, and again to go out and greet you!"

"So it might have been like this before you arrived this morning," Sam points out.

"I guess so," says the sergeant.

Gum whispers to his friends, "We all know who did this, right?"

"Vandals?" Egg says.

"Aliens," Gum says. "Now we have to prove it. Where should we start?"

TO TOUR THE HANGAR, TURN TO PAGE 12.
TO TOUR THE REC CENTER, TURN TO PAGE 14.
TO TOUR THE MEDICAL CENTER, TURN TO PAGE 16.

"We have to think like aliens," Gum says. He and his friends follow Ms. Marlow, Sergeant Houlihan, and two girls from the club.

"And how do we do that?" Egg asks. Cat and Sam laugh.

"If you're an alien," Gum says, "and you just escaped your cage at Zone 99, what's the first thing you do?"

"Try to get a guest spot on a late-night talk show?" Sam offers. Cat doubles over laughing.

"You try to find your ship," Gum says, "or build a new one."

"Of course," Egg says, shaking his head. "Why didn't I think of that?"

The group enters the old hangar by crossing a stretch of blacktop beyond the main building.

It looks run-down from the outside, but inside, the lights are bright and the exhibits are impressive. There's a long, sleek bomber, a pair of fighter jets, and a modern-looking drone that can be flown remotely.

One thing is missing, though.

"Sergeant," Gum says, using his most serious voice, "where are the other ships?"

"What other ships?" the sergeant asks.

Gum sidles up close and whispers loudly at her, "The *alien* ships."

The guide's face goes white for a moment. Then she laughs it off and leads the group along to the next section of the hangar.

Egg glares at Gum. "What did I do?" Gum protests.

The sergeant leads the group right past a door that reads: *Special Exhibit Storage: Do Not Enter*.

Gum stops short and grabs Egg's shirt. "Check it out," Gum says.

"Don't," Egg says.

But Gum is grinning and Sam is grinning. Even Cat seems to be growing a mischievous smile.

"Guys," Egg says. "We'll get in a *lot* of trouble."

"Won't it be worth it," Gum says, "if we crack this alien conspiracy wide open?"

TO GO IN, TURN TO PAGE 18.
TO STAY WITH THE GROUP, TURN TO PAGE 25.

The four junior detectives follow their club mates and the sergeant to the recreation center in the basement of the main building.

As they descend the stairwell, the fluorescent lights flicker and crackle. Cat grabs hold of Sam's arm, afraid.

But when they step into the rec center itself, the lights are bright and the cavernous room is filled with table tennis, foosball, and old arcade games. There's even an old empty pool behind a wall of windows.

"If we have some time at the end of the tour," says Sergeant Houlihan, "we might turn on the arcade games and let all you kids have a few free plays!"

Egg, Sam, Cat, and the other students cheer. Normally Gum would cheer with them, but his mind is elsewhere. Lining the ceiling above them as they move through the basement rec center is a large, metal duct.

"Guys," Gum says, grabbing the back of Egg's shirt. Cat and Sam stop, too.

Gum's eyes are still on the ducts above them. "Did you hear that?" he asks.

"Hear what?" Egg says.

"Thumping," Gum says. "Or bumping. Some scratching too. Maybe."

"You're losing it," Egg says. "And the tour is moving along without us."

Gum ignores him, though, and when the ducts move down a hall away from the tour, he follows the ducts.

"What are you doing?" Egg calls after him, but Sam and Cat hurry down the hall behind Gum. "Guys!"

"Something," Gum says, "or *someone* is in that duct, and it's going this way."

But at the end of the hallway is a wall with a single door. The duct goes right through to the other side. The door has a sign: *Tunnels to Barracks*.

To go through the door and check out the tunnel, turn to page 21.

To follow the group on the tour, turn to page 27.

"My theory is this," Gum says to his friends as they follow Sergeant Houlihan to the medical center. "What better place for the military to do experiments on aliens than here?" He grins.

"How about fantasyland?" Egg says.

Gum ignores him and hurries to the front of the group. "Sergeant," Gum says, "will you show us the secret lab where they examine the aliens?"

But the sergeant pretends not to hear him. "This hospital," she says, "was not only the medical wing of this base, but also the hospital for all veterans in the greater River City area."

"Wow," Egg says. "How did they have space?"

The sergeant smiles at him. "Well, they didn't," she admits. "That's why the new veterans' hospital was built downtown. Of course, once it was open, our little clinic wasn't much use."

"Except to help people on the base?" Cat asks.

The sergeant shakes her head. "By then, this base was not operational aside from the medical center," she says. "Once that closed, the base closed. It only reopened three years ago as the museum it is today."

"And the aliens," Gum says. "They obviously still live here."

The sergeant finally looks at Gum. "There are no aliens," she says firmly.

"Are they in the basement?" Gum asks.

"There. Are. No. Aliens!"

"Sub-basement?"

The sergeant marches off to continue the tour.

When she's out of earshot, Gum nods toward a door nearby marked *Stairwell*.

"No way," Egg says. "I'm not going anywhere to hunt for aliens. We'll stick with the tour."

Sam, though, crouches in front of the door. "I think we'd better do what Gum wants this time. Look."

Egg, Cat, and Gum step up next to her. Cut into the paint on the door are four long scratches — the scratches of a wicked claw.

To go through the door to investigate, turn to page 23.
To stick with the tour, turn to page 29.

"It's probably locked," Egg says, crossing his arms.

Gum grabs the handle and it opens with a satisfying click. He grins at Egg.

Egg scowls as Gum pulls the door open all the way.

Inside, the hallway is well lit by glaring fluorescent fixtures on the ceiling. The light reflects off the gleaming white floor and walls.

Along one side of the hall are huge windows, as if made to allow people walking down the hall to see what's going on inside each room beyond. But every room is completely dark, and seeing inside is impossible.

Gum hurries along the hall. Next to each dark window is a closed metal door, all of which are locked — except one.

"Guys," Gum says as he slowly pushes the door open. "This one isn't locked."

His three friends hurry down the hall to join him.

Gum steps slowly into the room. "We come in peace!" he calls into the darkness.

When Egg switches on the light, Gum jumps.

"No one's here," Egg says, moving past Gum. It's just an ordinary office, with an old metal desk and some file cabinets.

Gum sags with disappointment. "I thought there'd be cages with aliens in them," he admits.

Cat pats him on the back.

Sam walks to the desk and flips through the papers.

"Leave that stuff alone," Egg says. "There's no mystery here."

"Oh yeah?" Sam says, grinning. She holds up a file folder. "What's this?"

Gum grabs the folder and reads the label aloud: "UFOs?!"

Even Egg gasps.

Gum flips open the folder, but suddenly they hear a cough in the hallway.

"We have to hide!" Cat says as her eyes go wide.

"We have to *run*!" Sam says, grabbing the folder.

To take the file and run, turn to page 32.
To hide in the office, turn to page 48.

"I don't know if this is a good idea," Cat says, holding tight to Sam's arm.

Gum opens the door. Beyond the door are steep steps. The air is dusty and stale.

At the bottom of the steps is a long hallway, barely lit by a flickering fluorescent light on the ceiling.

"This must lead to the old barracks," Egg says. "I saw them as the bus pulled in. They're on the far side of the parking lot. This tunnel must be a half-mile long."

Sam peers down the hallway, but it's far too dark to see to the other end. "No one's been down here for ages," she says. Then she sneezes. "It's so dusty."

"Oh, yeah?" Gum says, scrambling past her. He grabs something off the floor. "Look at this!"

He holds up an apple core.

Cat sticks out her tongue and gags. "Gross," she says. "No thanks. It must have been here for years."

TURN THE PAGE.

Sam takes it from Gum and shakes her head. "No, it's pretty fresh. Like, this morning fresh. If it were very old, it'd be dry and brown."

"Oh, there's so much litter," Cat sighs, picking up a wrapper from the floor. "Look!"

"That's from a cheeseburger," Gum says, taking it from her. He sniffs the paper. "Still fresh."

"Then the vandals *did* come this way," Sam says.

"The aliens, you mean," Gum says. "Remember, we heard them in the vents. *Earthling* vandals don't travel through vents."

Sam taps her chin and says in a faraway voice, "Maybe so."

"And these footprints," Egg says, kneeling. He raises his camera and takes a few flash photos of the floor, lighting the hallway. "They're *definitely* not human."

Sam checks the photos. The prints have five fingers like a human hand, but the fingers are long and skinny, with a wicked claw at the end of each one.

To go back and report what they've found to the adults, turn to page 34.

To follow the tunnel to its end to catch the culprit, turn to page 52.

Cat shrieks. Egg gasps and snaps a photo of the scratches. Gum pulls a pack of strawberry-malted gum from his pocket and pops a piece in his mouth.

"You know," he says as he chews, "the door doesn't even say 'Do Not Enter' or anything like that. What's the big deal?"

He grabs the handle and pulls open the door.

Inside the stairwell the lights flicker, throwing the stairs into occasional darkness.

"I don't like this, you guys," Cat says as she and her friends descend.

"Wait a sec," Gum says, pulling out his phone. "Flashlight app." He clicks it on, and the stairwell lights up an eerie pale blue.

The stairs wind down to another door. A narrow window shows darkness beyond.

Sam throws open the door. "Come on," she says. "Bring that light."

Gum hurries after her and shines the light into the dark hallway, lighting a sign on the wall that reads, *Morgue*.

TURN THE PAGE.

"What does *mor-goo* mean?" he asks.

"Don't ask," Egg says as Cat enters the hallway behind the others.

"Don't ask what?" Cat says.

Egg knocks Gum's arm so the beam of his flashlight is off the sign. "Nothing, nothing!"

"I wonder," Gum says. "We saw that scratch on the door. Do you think that means the alien escaped from down here and is on the main floor . . . or came down here to hide and is here now?"

The beam of Gum's flashlight app dims and goes off.

"Uh-oh," Gum says, clicking the power button on his phone several times. "Dead battery."

From up ahead, they hear the scratch of claws on the cement floor. They freeze in place.

The scratching stops. An instant later they hear soft clicking and trilling.

"It's aliens," Gum says. "And they're *talking*."

TO INVESTIGATE THE NOISES, TURN TO PAGE 36.
TO RUN BACK UPSTAIRS, TURN TO PAGE 55.

By the time the junior detectives (and alien investigators) catch up with the group, Sergeant Houlihan is crouched beside a pedestal.

Atop the pedestal sits a scale model of a space shuttle. A little placard reads, *Space Shuttle* Columbia, *the first of its kind.*

"Why is she looking at the pedestal?" Gum asks. "Isn't the shuttle the important part here?"

The sergeant rises with a sigh and puts her hands on her hips. Shaking her head, she steps away from the pedestal.

The four sleuths gasp. The front of the gleaming black pedestal is marred by four long scratches.

"Claw marks!" Gum exclaims.

He stomps over to the sergeant. "Do you still deny there are aliens here on the base?" he says.

Sergeant Houlihan just rolls her eyes as she pulls out her cell phone. "I need to call maintenance," she says, then walks off.

TURN THE PAGE.

"Egg," Gum says. "Snap a photo. I'll write an exposé for the science club's blog. No! For the school paper. No! The *city* paper. This is big news."

Egg rolls his eyes, but he takes a couple of pictures anyway. It is a clue, after all.

"I don't think this is from an alien," Egg says, looking at his photos. "It could be anything. A wild animal."

"Why would a wild animal try to climb up this pedestal?" Gum says. He shakes his head. "No, this is an alien. He obviously saw the shuttle model and thought it was real. He planned to zoom up into space to go back home."

Before Egg can argue, Sam whistles to her friends from across the room.

"Guys!" Sam says, standing beside a door marked *Employee Break Room*.

Her three friends jog to her side. The break room door is scratched too, with the same long marks.

To follow Sam's clue, turn to page 68.
To stay with the group, turn to page 86.

Sergeant Houlihan stops and puts on a big smile. "This is the pool," she says. "At the far end of the room is a modest collection of exercise equipment as well."

Egg steps up to the edge of the empty pool. The water intakes and outputs at the bottom and on the sides of the pool are covered in a black mesh netting.

"Sergeant," he says. "What are those for?"

"Those keep the critters out," the sergeant says. "An old building like this with lots of empty pipes attracts a lot of . . . unwanted guests. Or it would, but we have that under control."

Gum is at the far end of the pool room, sneaking a look through a doorway.

"That," the sergeant says, hurrying over to him, "is the old canteen. Now it just has a couple of vending machines for museum patrons."

"Ooh," Gum says, rubbing his hands together. "I hope they have root beer gum. I've got a hankering."

TURN THE PAGE.

"Oh, I don't know," the sergeant says. "We'd better make sure it's okay with your teacher."

But Gum is already in the room, reaching into his pocket for a dollar bill.

Egg runs in too, because he has a hunch — and he's right. The room is a mess. Torn bags of chips, cheesy crumbs, and chocolate smears litter the floor and walls. The vending machine's side panel is nearly torn off.

"Oh, my," Sergeant Houlihan says. She pulls out her cell phone. "I'd better call maintenance."

Egg takes photos of the mess. He and Gum gather with Sam and Cat a few paces away.

"The alien did this!" Gum says. "He escaped through the ducts when he heard us coming."

"He?" Cat says, crossing her arms. "How do you know it wasn't 'she'?"

"Guys," Egg says. "It wasn't an alien. But I think I know who it was."

To take Egg's photos to Ms. Marlow in the hangar, turn to page 71.
To stay with the group, turn to page 89.

The sergeant leads the tour into a cold, well-lit room. A steel table sits in the middle of the room. Hanging on the wall are a stethoscope, an otoscope, and an X-ray image viewer.

"This is a typical examination room," the sergeant says. "There are two more just like it here in the medical wing."

As she rambles on, Sam whispers to her friends, "Booorrrrring."

"I wonder if my grandfather was ever in here," Egg says quietly.

"He was in the military?" Cat asks.

Egg nods. "He was stationed here for two years."

"If you'll all follow me this way . . . " the sergeant says, leading the students out of the exam room.

"I'll catch up," Egg tells his friends as they leave. "I want to get a few photos to show Gramps."

Egg takes several photos, being sure to get as many angles as possible in the hopes that Gramps will recognize something.

TURN THE PAGE.

"That ought to do it," Egg says, scrolling through his photos on the little display. As he does, something clanks and crashes in the corner of the exam room.

Egg flinches and crouches behind the exam table. "Hello?" he says.

It's quiet for a breathless moment. Egg rises from his hiding place — and the silence is cut by a ghastly scraping, clacking, and snarling, as something large and dark sprints from the room.

Egg runs back to his friends at the tail end of the group. "Did you see it?" he asks.

"See what?" Cat says.

"I . . . " Egg begins. "I don't know."

Gum's eyes go wide. "The alien," he says. "You saw it!"

"No," Egg says. "It wasn't an alien. But it was *something*."

"We should tell Sergeant Houlihan," Gum says.

"We should catch up to the group," Cat says.

TO TELL SERGEANT HOULIHAN, TURN TO PAGE 73.
TO FOLLOW THE GROUP, TURN TO PAGE 92.

"Just a second," Sam says, shoving the file folder into her shoulder bag. She bolts from the room. "This way!"

The four sleuths run deeper into the base, away from the sound of the cough.

Soon the hallway doubles around, forcing them to head back toward where they started.

Footsteps echo from up ahead, ringing through the labyrinth of turns and locked doors.

"Now what?" Gum says, bouncing on his toes. "We're so busted!"

Sam looks up and down the empty hallway as the echoing footsteps move slowly closer. A red light shines from around the corner, lighting the walls in a creepy glow.

"This way," she whispers.

Cat, Gum, and Egg sprint after Sam as she rounds the corner and slams palms-first into the push bar of an emergency-exit door.

The four stumble into the parking lot, and the emergency alarm screams.

The door catches as it swings closed, getting stuck a few inches open.

"Huh," Egg says, glancing at the stuck door. "Look at that."

The emergency door bursts open again, and Sergeant Houlihan and Ms. Marlow appear.

"What is going on?!" Ms. Marlow asks.

At the same moment, two uniformed men come running from the direction of the front gate. "What's with the sirens?" one of them asks.

Ms. Marlow, the sergeant, and the two base guards surround the four sleuths.

Their advisor puts her hands on her hips. "You four want to explain yourselves?"

"No need, Ms. M.!" Sam says. She reaches into her shoulder bag and pulls out the file folder labeled *UFOs*, then hands it to Ms. Marlow.

"What's this?" the advisor asks. "UFOs? Is this a joke?"

"Oh," says Sergeant Houlihan, reaching for the folder. "I can explain that."

Turn to page 38.

Cat sprints ahead of her friends. She almost stumbles at the bottom of the small set of steps leading back to the recreation room.

"Cat!" Sam says, hurrying after her. "Slow down!"

Cat barely gets her footing. She climbs the stairs more like a real cat, with the help of her front paws too.

"No way," she says. "I don't know what's down here, Sam, but it's not something I want to meet, especially in a dark, dusty, deserted hallway."

She reaches the door, throws it open, and steps into the bright white light of fluorescent fixtures.

And runs smack into Sergeant Houlihan. She stands there, hands on hips in her crisp military uniform, and cocks an eyebrow at Cat.

Sam, Egg, and Gum stumble out after Cat. The sergeant casts her meanest glare at them.

"Well?" Sergeant Houlihan says.

"It doesn't say 'Do Not Enter,'" Gum quickly points out.

The sergeant narrows her eyes at him and looks at Cat. "Well?" Sergeant Houlihan says again.

"To be honest, Sergeant," Cat says, "we heard a noise in the vent."

Cat looks up at the shiny metal duct above them.

"So we followed it through this door," Cat says. "Just to see where the ducts go, I mean."

"She means, to follow the escaped alien," Gum says, smiling.

"Not this again," the sergeant says.

"Do you continue to deny the existence of extraterrestrial life-forms on this base?" Gum says, leaning in.

Before the sergeant can even reply, Gum goes on. "And do you further deny that scientists on this base, probably including *you*, have been experimenting on those life-forms since the 1940s?"

"I'm only twenty-eight," the sergeant says.

TURN TO PAGE 42.

Cat holds tight to Sam's hand as the four move deeper into the dark hallway.

Up ahead, the trilling stops, replaced by the sound of claws scraping on the tile floor as the creatures ahead scurry deeper into the basement hallways.

"They're getting away!" Gum says, and darkness or not, he sprints off down the hall.

"Wait!" Cat says, holding Sam's hand even tighter to stop her braver friend from leaving her alone in the dark.

She doesn't need to worry, though, because moments later there's a crash up ahead.

"Ow." It's Gum.

The others hurry ahead and find him. Though there's very little light, they see at once that he's been stopped by a pile of junk: old aluminum desks, a knocked-over floor lamp, and a pair of old wheelchairs, folded and lying on their sides.

Beyond that, there are cardboard file boxes stacked so high they practically form a wall.

Sam peers at the debris. "There are some gaps," she says. "I can see through it a bit. Whatever is making those sounds must be smaller than us."

"Aliens," Gum says. "Small aliens."

Cat backs away from the debris. "OK," she says. "They got away. Darn! I guess we'd better get back upstairs. You know, where there's light and more people and . . . light."

"Maybe Cat's right," Egg says. "I'm not feeling totally safe down here, and — "

"Wait a second!" Gum suddenly shouts. He stands next to Sam, and they're squinting into the darkness beyond the debris. "I see something. It looks like . . . like — "

"Eyes!" Sam says. "Two of them . . . I mean, four."

"The alien has *four eyes*," Gum says, his voice urgent and awed.

"No, Gum," Sam says. "There are two of them. That makes four."

"Let me see," Egg says, letting his curiosity get the best of him. "Ooh, they're yellow."

TURN TO PAGE 45.

"Just a second," Ms. Marlow says, turning away from Sergeant Houlihan. She flips the folder open.

"Please," the sergeant says. "That's not for you."

"Is that right?" Ms. Marlow says.

The sergeant reaches for the folder, but Ms. Marlow drops it onto the parking lot blacktop.

Everyone — except Sergeant Houlihan — gasps as they look down at the short stack of fallen papers. The top one is a photograph.

A photograph of an alien.

"I knew it!" Gum says.

He grabs the photo for a closer look. His friends look over his shoulder.

"Wow," Cat says, her eyes wide as she stares down at the photo. "That's an alien?"

It's standing between two men in old-fashioned military uniforms, but it's only about half as tall as they are.

Its eyes and head are huge. Its long arms are skinny as twigs, and its legs end in long, flat feet.

"You have to show us," Gum says, looking up at the sergeant. "Now that the truth is out in the open, you might as well."

Sergeant Houlihan looks up into the blue sky and groans. "It's not an alien," she says.

"You're still denying it?" Gum says. "Even after we found the photo?"

He scoops up the rest of the papers. "And what about all this other stuff?" he says, shuffling through the papers. But as he looks, his face falls.

There are more photos of aliens, along with copies of posters for sci-fi movies from decades past, and yellowed clippings from newspapers with headlines like *Farmer Sees UFO* and *Local Woman Marries Martian!*

"Wait a second," Gum says, handing the papers to the sergeant. "What *is* all this stuff?"

"As I've been trying to tell you," Sergeant Houlihan says, "there are no aliens. But we *are* planning an exhibit about *made-up* aliens."

TURN THE PAGE.

"Oh," Gum says. "So all this stuff is . . . fake?"

The sergeant sighs. "Yes," she says. "Now you're getting it."

"I told you," Egg says, eyebrows raised.

"In that case," Ms. Marlow says, "we come to the matter of you four separating from the group, snooping in off-limits offices, and, finally, setting off the alarm by using an emergency exit door."

"Oh," Gum says. "That."

"Don't tell us," Sam says, putting up her hands before Ms. Marlow can continue. "We spend the rest of the field trip on the bus?"

Ms. Marlow nods, and the four friends walk dejectedly to the bus.

"With the bus driver, Smelly Mel," Egg says.

"Just please tell me he's not having salami and horseradish again," Cat says. "I swear, I had to wash my sweater three times to get that stink out!"

THE END

To follow another path, turn to page 11.

Egg sighs and steps in front of Gum to speak to the sergeant. "We found garbage: apple cores, candy wrappers . . . that sort of thing. We suspect whoever vandalized the museum probably escaped that way."

"And by 'whoever,' he means the aliens," Gum says, gently shoving Egg aside.

The sergeant crosses her arms and glares.

"Uh-oh," Cat says, moving up next to Sam. "I think she's gonna blow."

"Honest, Sergeant," Egg says. "We're trying to solve this case. I don't believe in aliens, promise."

Gum catches the sergeant's eye and winks.

"That's it!" the sergeant says. "Ms. Marlow! Ms. Marlow!"

Their advisor sticks her head into the corridor from the pool room nearby. "Yes? Anything wrong?"

"I have had enough of these four troublemakers," she says.

Ms. Marlow sigh. "What did they do now?"

The sergeant runs down the list of crimes: straying from the tour, entering off-limits areas — even though Gum protests that no sign was posted — and spreading wild rumors about aliens.

"Is this true?" Ms. Marlow says.

Gum and Sam begin to argue, but Cat puts a hand on each of their arms.

"It is true, Ms. Marlow," Cat says. "We're sorry."

Gum starts to protest, but Cat cuts him off again, "We're *all* very sorry."

Ms. Marlow gives the four of them a long, hard stare. "Sorry to do this, kids," she says. "I know you've been excited about this field trip."

"Oh, no," Gum says in a cold, frightened whisper. "Please not Smelly Mel . . ."

"But you'll have to spend the rest of the time on the bus," Ms. Marlow says.

"Oh, no!" Gum says, a little louder.

"Mel the bus driver will keep an eye on you," Ms. Marlow says.

TURN THE PAGE.

Gum drops to his knees and bellows toward the ceiling, "Nooo!"

Five minutes later, the four junior detectives climb aboard the bus. Mel sits in his driver's seat, a metal box on his lap.

"Hey, kids," he says, grinning down at them as they board. "I was just about to have some lunch. Hope you don't mind!"

By the time they reach their seats at the back of the bus, the smell of Mel's sandwich fills the air.

"What are you having today, Mel?" Gum asks, frowning at his friends.

"Let's see," Mel says, peering down at his thick, sopping-wet sandwich. "Today I've got tongue on pumpernickel, with bleu cheese. Mm-mm!"

Gum slouches in his seat. He groans and whispers, "See, Cat? Running into aliens in a dark basement hallway would have been a pleasure compared to this!"

THE END

TO FOLLOW ANOTHER PATH, TURN TO PAGE 11.

"Can we *please* go upstairs before they see us?" Cat pleads, louder now, grabbing her friends' shirts to pull them away from the debris.

"Too late," Egg says, as the two sets of eyes suddenly seem to focus on the sleuths like lasers.

"Maybe they're friendly?" Gum says.

Then, as if a switch has been hit, the foul things charge, clicking, hissing, and trilling.

"They're not friendly," Sam says calmly.

"Run!" Gum says, finally turning from the debris. He knocks right into Cat, sending them both sprawling to the floor.

Sam lifts Cat by the elbow and pulls her along. "Come on, you two!" she calls over her shoulder to Gum and Egg.

The four friends sprint back up the dark hallway.

Cat stumbles over Sam's feet, and the two of them fall. Gum and Egg trip over their friends, and the four detectives lie helpless on the floor.

With no other options, Egg raises his camera.

TURN THE PAGE.

"Close your eyes!" he shouts, and he snaps photo after photo, illuminating the dark with his flash.

No sounds come from the hallway, except the heavy breathing of the four detectives.

"I think you scared them off," Sam says, sitting up and pushing her hair out of her face.

"Is it safe?" Cat says. She sits up as her friends get to their feet.

Egg reaches down to help Cat up.

"I think so," Egg says. He pats his camera and grins. "The light scared them off."

Together, the friends find the stairwell and start up. At the first landing, Sam stops and grabs Egg's arm.

"Wait a second," Sam says. "What about the photos?"

"Oh!" Egg says. "I only wanted to scare them off. I didn't even think of the photos!"

The four friends huddle together in the half-light of the stairwell as Egg clicks on the display. No one says anything for a minute.

Then Gum says, "So . . . they weren't chasing us? The aliens?"

Egg sighs and clicks off the display. "I don't think they were aliens. I think they were raccoons."

"And I don't think they were chasing us," Cat says. Then she grins. "But it *was* fun pretending it might be aliens, I have to admit."

"I don't think Gum was pretending," Sam says.

Egg shrugs. "I think the museum staff will have enough to worry about with two raccoons on the loose. We should probably go tell them."

Gum says, "Sure. Let's go tell them about the 'raccoons.'" He makes quotation marks with his hands and winks at Cat. The whole group snickers.

THE END

TO FOLLOW ANOTHER PATH, TURN TO PAGE 11.

"Let's get out of here!" Gum says.

"It's too late to run," Egg says. "Whoever's out there might be blocking the only way out."

"Then we'll have to hide, I guess," Sam says.

Cat opens the closet door. It's dark inside, and messy, but she steps in and moves to the back.

"In here!" she whispers loudly.

The others squeeze in. It's a tight fit.

"Everyone be quiet," Sam whispers.

They're crammed in so tightly that Cat can hear her friends breathing.

"Hopefully whoever is out there will pass by quickly," Sam whispers.

Cat holds her breath and listens. She can just make out uneven footsteps. They sound like they're still out in the hallway.

The footsteps are accompanied by a rising and falling squeak and a sloshing sound.

"Whoa," Gum says suddenly, his voice far too loud.

The others hiss at him: "Shh!"

"But look what I found!" Gum insists, whispering now, but still too loudly.

"Just be quiet," Sam whispers. "Another minute, that's all."

But Gum clicks on his phone and shines its light at the object in his hand.

They all gasp: it's a shining metal ray gun.

"Wow," Sam says. "Let me see that."

Sam takes the ray gun and feels the weight of it in her hand. It's long and gleaming. Its tip is circled by three translucent red rings.

"It looks just like the ray guns in the old movies Grandpa loves," Sam says, her voice full of wonder.

When she taps a small button on its side, each circle on the ray gun's body begins to glow.

"Whoa, turn it off!" Gum says, almost shouting now. "It's real!"

Cat backs deeper into the closet, knocking into what feel like heavy coats.

TURN THE PAGE.

"Shine the light over here," Cat says.

Gum shines his phone's light toward Cat. Behind her hang several shining silver outfits — space suits. On the floor beneath them sit three helmets with red visors.

"Wow," Gum says. "These must be what the aliens were wearing when the base caught them."

"Quiet!" Egg whispers. "The footsteps are close!"

But his friends are too excited. Gum and Sam grab a space suit each to hold up to themselves.

"I think this one would fit me!" Sam says. "A little baggy, maybe."

Cat, meanwhile, grabs the helmet at her foot and plops it on her head. "Check me out!" she says, her voice muffled through the helmet's visor.

"Guys!" Egg hisses. "They're right outside."

Gum finally hears him. "What if it's the aliens?" he asks Sam.

Sam's mouth drops open. "They could be coming here . . . to get their stuff."

TURN TO PAGE 58.

"I don't see how we have any real choice," Sam says, her hands on her hips. In the near dark, to Cat, she looks very impressive: tall and almost menacing, the deep shadows on her face giving her a sinister air.

"We have to go on, deeper into the belly of the base," Sam goes on, her chin high, "if we're going to solve this case."

Gum gapes for a moment. "You're so weird," he finally says.

Sam winks, and the four friends move along the underground corridor.

"This might help," Gum says, pulling his cell phone from his pocket and shining its light along the hall.

It's a sloppy mess, but there are no aliens up ahead. The hall goes on a long way, its walls bare, aside from switched-off or long-dead wall sconces.

At the hall's end, the kids almost stumble as they reach the bottom of a set of stairs leading up.

"To the barracks, I guess?" Egg says, slowly starting up the stairs.

The others follow, Gum lighting the way with his phone's flashlight app. Halfway up, though, the light goes dim and then switches off completely.

"Oops," Gum says, thumping the phone against the palm of his other hand. "Forgot to plug it in last night. Battery's dead."

Gum's voice is light and good-humored, but in the fresh darkness, the kids can see even less than they could before he pulled out his phone.

Cat holds Sam's hand as they finish the climb.

Egg grips the bannister with one hand and steadies the camera around his neck with the other.

A pair of steel doors stands open before them, and beyond that is a wide-open space.

The little bit of light sneaks in through windows covered with blinds, curtains, and old furniture pushed against the wall, as if set aside and discarded.

TURN THE PAGE.

"This must be the lounge," Sam says, stepping into the cavernous room.

"My grandfather was stationed here as a young man," Egg says. "I bet he hung out here."

He raises his camera and snaps a few photos. "He'll want to see these," he says, "even if we're not supposed to be here."

Cat stays close to Sam. Together they prowl through the lounge. Sam looks for clues. Cat listens and looks, ever on edge, worried someone — or something — will jump out at any moment.

When the metal blinds across the lounge shake, Cat jumps, shrieks, and grabs hold of Sam's arm.

Sam shushes her. "It's over there!" she whispers to Gum.

Gum nods.

Egg moves slowly forward, his camera up.

As they get close, they hear a chattering and a very fast clicking.

"What is that?" Egg says. "It seems familiar."

Gum shakes his head. "They're talking."

TURN TO PAGE 62.

Shrieking wildly, Cat leads her friends in a sprint back to the stairwell.

"I can't see anything!" Cat says, feeling around on the wall for a door handle. "Oh, is this it?"

She tries the door, but it's locked.

Her friends catch up. Sam takes her arm and says, "This way. The stairwell is across the hall."

"Are you sure?" Cat says. "I thought we came from this way."

"I don't think so," Egg says, trying to pull Cat away from the locked door.

"Wait," Cat says. "What does this sign say?"

She opens her eyes wide, trying to read the white letters in the dark. "Mor-goo?" she says. "What's mor-goo?"

"It's nothing," Egg says. "Just come *on*."

But like a flash it hits her: it doesn't say "mor-goo." It says *morgue*.

A chill crosses her shoulders like an icy draft. She gasps.

TURN THE PAGE.

Quick-thinking Sam covers Cat's wide-open mouth with her hand before Cat can let out a wail. With Egg's help, the two of them pull Cat away from the terrifying door and through another door to the stairwell, which Gum holds open for them.

Cat is nearly shaking when they reach the top of the steps. There, some light sneaks in from the bright hallway of the medical wing.

"First aliens," she says, almost stuttering. "Then *dead bodies*." She shivers again.

"Cat," Egg says, "I doubt very much that the morgue here has been used for a very long time."

"Unless it's where they're keeping the alien bodies," Gum says, stroking his chin. "We should probably pick the lock."

"Gum!" Cat snaps, spinning on him as Sam pulls open the stairwell door.

Standing there with her arms crossed, and wearing a powerful glare, is Sergeant Houlihan.

Behind her is Ms. Marlow, and standing around them in a half circle is the rest of the science club.

"Oh," Cat says, looking up sheepishly. "Hi."

"We can explain," Egg starts, but Gum cuts him off.

"Fine," he says, stepping up to the sergeant and Ms. Marlow, "we're in trouble. Big whoop."

"Big," Sergeant Houlihan says, "*whoop*?"

"Exactly," Gum says, grinning up at her. "Because we *saw* the aliens."

The sergeant's face goes red. "Nonsense," she says angrily.

"You . . . you," Ms. Marlow says, looking Gum square in the eyes. The teacher's voice quivers and quakes as she finishes. "You saw them?"

"Well," Gum says, averting his eyes a moment. "We definitely *heard* them. I might have seen something. It's hard to say."

"It was pretty dark," Egg confirms.

"Cat was practically hysterical," Gum says.

"I wasn't!" Cat says.

TURN TO PAGE 65.

"Before they find their ship and fly back home!" Gum says.

The footsteps stop with a squeak and start again, along with the rising and falling whine and the gross-sounding slosh.

It's in the room now — the footsteps, and whatever foul creature produces them.

Cat catches her breath and grabs Sam's hand.

Sam clutches her silver space suit.

Gum faces the inside of the closet door and slips his phone back into his pocket. He raises the ray gun and points it, ready to defend his friends and himself against the approaching aliens.

Egg moves deeper into the closet.

The office light clicks on. The footsteps move closer. They sound uneven, inhuman.

The feet stop just outside the closet, blocking a bit of the light sneaking in under the door.

Gum's finger twitches on the trigger of the ray gun.

The door swings open.

The kids scream.

Gum pulls the trigger. The ray gun lights up and a siren blares from the little speakers on each side of its body: *Wee-oooo-weee-oooo-weee-oooo . . . !*

Standing there is the museum janitor.

"What are you kids doing in there?" the janitor says, looking confused. He reaches out, snatches the ray gun, and clicks a switch on the underside of its grip. The lights and siren stop. "This room is off limits to guests."

"Is it?" Sam says, moving toward the door, urging her friends on with her. "We must have gotten lost. Sorry! We'll find our way back to the group now."

But Sergeant Houlihan stands in the office doorway, stopping them in their tracks.

"There you four are," she says. "I knew you were trouble."

The four friends skulk past her to find Ms. Marlow waiting in the hallway.

TURN THE PAGE.

"What if we told you we found a bunch of real alien technology in the closet in there?" Gum asks.

"What you found," the sergeant says, as the group moves back toward the museum proper, "was part of an exhibit opening next month about the history of aliens in science fiction."

"So those were . . . movie props?" Sam asks.

"That's right," the sergeant says.

"That's pretty cool too," Sam says. "I'll ask my grandpa to take me to the exhibit!"

"Oh, no," says the sergeant. "The four of you are not allowed here again for a long, long time."

Ms. Marlow escorts the four friends onto the bus. "You'll wait here," she says, "until the field trip is over."

Mel the bus driver smiles down at them. "Welcome, kids," he says, holding a slimy sandwich. "Anyone hungry?"

THE END

TO FOLLOW ANOTHER PATH, TURN TO PAGE 11.

"In clicks?" Cat whispers.

The clicks become faster and more urgent. Then there's a high whine, like a tiny machine starting up, and more clicking.

"That's probably their communicator," Gum suggests. "Like a walkie-talkie to their mother ship."

"Mother ship?" Sam says, cocking an eyebrow at him.

"Sure," Gum says. "Did you think they'd be able to take one of the old airplanes here all the way back to their galaxy? Don't be ridiculous!"

"Right," Egg says, rolling his eyes. "Don't be ridiculous."

"The mother ship will pick them up any minute, I bet," Gum says, crossing his arms. "You watch."

"Oh, we'll watch," Egg says, grinning.

The clicking stops. The lounge fills with an eerie, heavy silence as the four detectives stand close together in the middle of the room, waiting, listening, barely breathing.

"Any minute, huh?" Egg says after a long while.

But just then, the roar of an engine shatters the silence. Soon bright lights fill the wall of shuttered windows at the front of the lounge.

The lounge floods with white and orange light. Particles of dust catch the light and reflect, so they seem to be a million tiny fairies, fluttering among the friends.

"Whoa," Sam says.

"I told you," Gum whispers.

"It's so beautiful," Cat says.

The lounge doors burst open — but no aliens appear, ready to take their stolen comrades back to their home galaxy.

"How did you kids get in here?" shouts a man in an Air Force security uniform. He and his partner shine high-powered flashlights in their faces. "The door was locked," he continues, clicking off his flashlight and striding across the room.

Egg looks through the open front doors. Two security cars, their white and orange lights shining right into the windows, are parked just outside.

TURN THE PAGE.

"You'd better come with us," the guard says.

Ms. Marlow is furious as she leads the four sleuths across the parking lot.

"No matter how many times I say it," she mumbles angrily, "kids just cannot comprehend 'stay with your group.'"

"We're sorry, Ms. Marlow," Cat says.

"We are," Gum says. "We really are. But you *have* to listen to us. The escaped aliens are in the lounge. We followed them there."

"Tracked them, really," Sam says.

"We heard them talking to the mother ship," Gum says. "If we don't do something right away, we could be looking at a full-scale invasion of Earth!"

Ms. Marlow puts her face in her hands. "On the bus," she mutters. "Just get on the bus and wait for the field trip to be over. All four of you."

THE END

To follow another path, turn to page 11.

The sergeant stands tall and crosses her arms. She looks each of the four sleuths in the eye before settling on Sam. "What did *you* see?"

"Me?" Sam says. "Nothing."

The sergeant smiles. "See?" she says, looking briefly at Ms. Marlow. "These four children went where they knew they were not permitted to go."

"There was no 'Do Not Enter' sign," Gum says.

The sergeant continues, talking right over him. "And now they hope to distract us by claiming to have seen *aliens*," she says. "It's patently absurd, and they must be disciplined at once."

"Okay, we didn't see anything," Gum admits, "but we did hear them."

"That's true," Sam says.

"And what do *aliens* sound like?" the sergeant asks, smiling smugly.

Gum, Sam, Egg, and Cat all try to answer at once. Clicking, tongue waggling, trilling . . . all manner of wild noises echoing up and down the gleaming medical wing hallway.

TURN THE PAGE.

Finally the sergeant throws up her hands and shouts, "Quiet, quiet, quiet!"

The junior detectives quiet down. After a beat, Gum says, "Well, you asked."

"I've heard enough," the sergeant says. She turns to Ms. Marlow. "I insist the four of them leave the tour *permanently*."

Ms. Marlow sighs. "All right," she says. "Come on, you four."

Gum stomps his feet, crosses his arms, and stands firmly where he is. "No way," he says. "I'm not going *anywhere* until *she* admits there are aliens loose in the basement."

"Ridiculous," the sergeant says as she leads the rest of the students away to continue the tour.

"This isn't over!" Gum says.

"Come *on*," Cat says, taking Gum by the elbow.

Egg takes his other elbow, and together they manage to pull him along.

"You haven't heard the end of James 'Gum' Shoo," he shouts.

His friends lead him away. "I'll tell the world about the cover-up!" he shouts more loudly, craning his head around to yell down the hall.

"I'm sure everyone will believe you," Egg says.

As they climb aboard the bus to wait till the field trip is over, Mel the bus driver smiles down at them.

The kids smile and try not to look at his latest gross sandwich. They find seats at the back.

Gum slumps in his seat.

"Gum, do you really think there were aliens down there?" Cat asks quietly.

Gum thinks a moment. Then he shrugs. "I don't know," he admits. "But I hope there were."

His friends sit quietly for a minute. Sam nods.

Cat smiles.

Egg shrugs and says, "Yeah, me, too."

THE END

TO FOLLOW ANOTHER PATH, TURN TO PAGE 11.

"I don't think we're supposed to go in there," Cat says, nodding toward the sign.

"It doesn't say not to," Gum points out. "In fact, as a paying guest of the museum — "

"We didn't pay anything," Egg points out.

" — I'm very interested in learning about employee break rooms," Gum finishes. "Perhaps this museum has a break room exhibit."

He looks at the door and its sign as if seeing them for the first time. "Ah! This must be it!" he says, and, grinning at Egg, throws open the door.

"Wow," Egg says, looking over Gum's shoulder. He snaps a few photos.

The break room, which looks kind of like a large kitchen, is a total mess. The fridge stands open, its contents spilled across the floor, its light the only light in the room.

Sam steps into the break room. "This is good," Sam says, stepping carefully over an overturned egg carton.

"How so?" Egg says. He follows her in and snaps photos of the wreckage.

"I see coffee grounds," Sam explains, "spilled sugar, lots of sticky eggs. That means we'll find lots of good evidence in here."

"Like fingerprints?" Cat asks. She gingerly steps into the room behind Gum and stays close to the wall. Her back knocks against the light switch, and the ceiling fixture turns on. "Oh!"

"Ah, thanks, Cat," Sam says, winking at her.

Gum squats beside a puddle of egg yolk, mixed up with spilled coffee grounds. It forms a muddy-looking goop. But what catches his eye are the tracks.

"Sam, check this out," he says. "Footprints — and they're not from anyone's shoe."

Sam squats beside him. The prints are small, but look a lot like a person's handprints. Except they're longer and skinnier.

"Longer and skinnier," Sam mutters aloud, thinking.

Gum nods. "Just like an alien," he says.

TURN TO PAGE 75.

"I know you guys are counting on an alien adventure on this trip," Egg says as he leads the way from the old rec center to the hangar, where Ms. Marlow is leading a small tour of her own. "But I don't think anything extraterrestrial is responsible for the wreckage at the museum this morning," he finishes.

The kids cross a small gravel patio and enter the hangar. Before they spot Ms. Marlow, they reach a pedestal. On top of it sits a scale model of a space shuttle.

"Look at this," Egg says, crouching next to the pedestal. He takes a few photos of it.

"Pretty sure the exhibit is the shuttle on top of it, Egg," Sam says, elbowing Gum.

"Look closer," Egg insists, stepping away to make room.

Sam peers at the spot on the pedestal. "Claw marks," she says. "Good eye."

"I'm a photographer," Egg says. "We have to have good eyes."

TURN THE PAGE.

Gum takes a look too. "So much for your theory," Gum says. "This proves it was aliens."

Egg wrinkles his brow at Gum. "How so?" he asks.

"Simple," Gum says haughtily. "Any clawed creature trying to reach a small space shuttle is probably a small creature *from space*."

"That," Egg says, "is the most ridiculous thing I've ever heard."

Their teacher's voice echoes from deeper inside the hangar.

"There's Ms. Marlow," Egg says. "Come on."

The four sleuths hurry through the huge building, dodging around exhibits of shuttles, satellites, and even old supersonic airplanes.

"Ms. Marlow!" Egg calls, jogging the last few yards to their advisor.

"Edward," Ms. Marlow says, using Egg's real name. "Aren't you supposed to be with Sergeant Houlihan in the rec center?"

She spots Cat, Gum, and Sam behind Egg.

TURN TO PAGE 79.

"Egg," Sam says, giving him a stern look, "if you saw something in that exam room, we have to investigate."

Egg shakes his head. "I'm not going back in there," he says.

"Me neither," Cat says. "Let's go tell Sergeant Houlihan."

Sam gives both her friends a long look. "Fine," she finally says. "If you two are convinced it's dangerous, we'll go straight to an adult."

The four friends hurry along the hallway and find their fellow students and Sergeant Houlihan standing at the window of a surgical bay.

Egg hurries up to the sergeant. "Sorry," he says. "It's an emergency."

"Right," Gum says. "The escaped aliens are in the examination room back there."

Egg quickly interjects, "He's kidding! Look, I don't know what's in there, but something is."

He explains how he stayed behind to take photos and ran out when something moved.

TURN THE PAGE.

"You shouldn't have been in there on your own," the sergeant says. Then she sighs. "Fine," she says. "Everyone, this way."

She leads the tour back toward the exam room, where the door is standing wide open.

"In there?" she asks.

Egg nods. "Just a few minutes ago," he says.

"You kids wait here," the sergeant says.

She moves closer to the exam room door. She presses herself against the wall. Then she takes two deep breaths and spins into the room.

"Don't move!" she shouts into the room. "You're under . . . arrest?"

The four investigators exchange a glance and hurry up to the exam room doorway.

Inside, the exam room is a total mess. Posters are torn, equipment is broken and scattered across the floor.

A glass vial has fallen from the counter and shattered.

TURN TO PAGE 82.

"Now you know what alien footprints look like?" Egg says, shaking his head in disbelief.

"That's what they always look like," Gum says, adding quickly, "in movies and stuff."

Sam stands up and keeps her eyes on the floor as she follows the funny-looking footprints around the kitchen. They cross the floor, climb up a fallen chair to the table, and make the short hop to the counter.

The tracks slip down from the counter and enter the fridge before darting across the room toward a door. It's marked *Pantry*, and it stands slightly open.

Sam nods toward the door. "Whatever it is," she whispers, "it's still here."

Cat almost shrieks, but catches herself and snaps her mouth shut. She ends up making a squealing hum noise instead.

"Shh . . ." Sam says, putting her finger to her lips. She tiptoes toward the open door.

Gum joins her, and Egg stands a few paces back, camera raised.

TURN THE PAGE.

As Sam and Gum get closer, they hear grumbling and rummaging, the sounds of plastic bags of food, and of snarfing and chewing and gobbling.

"It's in there!" Gum whispers urgently.

I know! Sam mouths back to him.

She shushes him again, grabs the door handle, and mouths, *One, two, three!*

Sam throws open the door, and she and Gum stand in the open doorway. Egg stands a few paces behind them, his camera flash firing wildly, and Cat is behind him and on her toes to see better.

Looking back at them, its beady eyes red and wild, its little hands wrapped around a half-unwrapped chocolate bar, and its distinctive fur pattern just like a burglar's mask, is a big, fat raccoon.

It opens its mouth wide, and screams.

Sam screams back — before she slams the pantry door and the four junior detectives tear from the room.

"Ms. Marlow!" Gum shouts.

"Sergeant Houlihan!" Egg shouts.

Up ahead, the tour group stops and turns around.

"Raccoon!" Sam, Egg, Gum, and Cat all shout together.

The sergeant calls animal control and they catch the raccoon and release it in the woods.

"It's that stuck door, I bet," Egg says. "It wasn't open very far, but far enough for that raccoon to squeeze inside."

The sergeant crosses her arms and grins at Gum. "Are you convinced there are no aliens here now?" she asks.

Gum snorts. "With the door propped open all night, they probably slipped out hours ago."

The sergeant groans and stomps away.

Gum looks at Egg, Sam, and Cat and asks, "What did I say?"

THE END

TO FOLLOW ANOTHER PATH, TURN TO PAGE 11.

"Oh, I see," she says, mild irritation in her voice. "Are we solving a mystery this morning?"

Egg feels his face go warm. "Well," he says, "something like that — with your help."

"My help?" Ms. Marlow says, all irritation gone. She smiles. "Well, when you put it *that* way . . . ."

Egg switches on his camera's display and brings up his most recent photos: the scratches on the pedestal and the tracks in the vending machine room back in the rec center.

"Didn't you tell us you know a lot about animal tracks?" Egg asks as his friends reach him and stand behind him.

"Oh, yeah!" Cat says excitedly. "You were a park ranger after college, right?"

Ms. Marlow smiles. "Yes," she says. "I'm pleased you remember that!"

"Well," Egg says, turning the display to face Ms. Marlow, "what do you make of these?"

TURN THE PAGE.

Ms. Marlow furrows her brow and takes the camera from Egg. She clicks through the photos.

"Small prints," she says. "Five distinct fingers on the hands. Elongated feet, also with five digits. Almost human-looking. There's only one possible answer in this region."

"Aliens," Gum says.

Ms. Marlow smirks at him. "Raccoons."

"I thought so!" Egg says. "My guess is they came in through the stuck emergency door Sergeant Houlihan told us about," Egg says. "And Gum heard one in the ducts over the rec center."

"Thank you, Edward," Ms. Marlow says. "We need animal control, it seems."

After a quick call, two county workers arrive and catch a raccoon in the employee break room and one in the old dormitory.

As the science club students climb onto the bus at the end of the trip, Egg turns to Gum. "Sorry, Gum," Egg says. "I know you were hoping to find aliens today."

Ms. Marlow, standing beside the bus door, smiles.

Gum shrugs. "The existence of raccoons does not disprove the existence of aliens," he says. "I have not lost faith."

"That's a very mature response," Ms. Marlow says, "if a little delusional."

Gum slides into his seat at the back of the bus and his three best friends join him, laughing.

Cat notices Gum is actually glum. While Egg and Sam joke, Cat nudges him. "Hey, you never know. Maybe they were *alien* raccoons."

Gum is quiet for a minute and then his eyes light up. "That *is* a perfect disguise for an alien — no one would ever know!"

Cat winks at him and the two of them share a smile.

THE END

To follow another path, turn to page 11.

Sergeant Houlihan stands just inside, her hand on her forehead. When the four friends fill the doorway behind her, she turns.

Her face is red. "What happened in here?" she asks.

"Like I said," Egg says, "I saw . . . oh."

It dawns on Egg that the sergeant isn't angry at whatever creature destroyed the exam room. She saw the wrecked room, looked at Egg and his friends, and decided *they* were the vandals.

"Wait a minute," Egg says, backing up a little. "We didn't do it!"

The sergeant puts her fists on her hips. "You admitted that you stayed in the room without supervision after the tour had moved on," the sergeant points out.

"Well, yes, but I was just — " Egg starts, but the sergeant cuts him off just as Ms. Marlow appears with the rest of the science club.

"Ah!" the sergeant says. "Ms. Marlow, just the person I wanted to see. Take a look at this."

Ms. Marlow sticks her head inside the exam room door. "Oh my goodness," she says. "My kids didn't do this, did they?"

"Unless I hear a better explanation . . ." Sergeant Houlihan says.

"How about the escaped aliens?" Gum says.

The sergeant keeps her eyes on Ms. Marlow and says, "Which sounds more likely to you? An escaped alien or four troublemakers?"

Ms. Marlow stammers, "I . . . well . . . I suppose troublemakers?"

"Exactly," the sergeant says. "Please remove these kids from the tour."

Ms. Marlow sighs. "Come on, kids," she says.

As Ms. Marlow leads the four junior detectives out of the museum, they pass under a series of ducts.

Egg grabs Gum's arm. "Hey, listen," Egg says.

The four friends stand stock still and look up at the duct.

TURN TO PAGE 85.

There's a scraping sound, like someone is crawling around in there.

They follow under the duct for a few paces until they reach a vent. Inside the duct is total blackness, but as they look up, suddenly two little red eyes stare back at them.

They gasp.

"Hey!" Ms. Marlow snaps at them from farther along the hallway. "What are you guys waiting for?" she says. "Come on!"

"But we saw . . ." Egg begins to say, but when he looks up at the vent again, the red eyes are gone. "Oh, never mind."

"Good," Ms. Marlow says, hurrying them along. "I hope you four will remember this and stay out of trouble for a while."

But the field trip mystery friends would remember only one thing from this trip: that wicked-looking pair of eyes, staring down at them.

THE END

TO FOLLOW ANOTHER PATH, TURN TO PAGE 11.

"I feel like we're missing a lot," Sam says, shoving her hands in her pockets. "We've seen several clues, but we haven't followed up on any of them."

The sergeant leads the tour through a large, dark doorway into a gallery lit only by lighted signs and backlit exhibits.

"I'll give you a few minutes to look around," the sergeant says. "Then there's a short film about the base's history."

The four friends stick together in the dark.

There are scale models of old-fashioned airplanes and fighter jets. There's even a scale model of the Air Force base itself.

"So we would be right around . . ." Egg says, leaning over the base model, "there." He points to a spot at the rear of the hangar.

Just then, Sam sneezes. She is not a dainty sneezer, and half the room jumps.

A shadowy figure scurries along the wall behind the model of the Air Force base.

Cat shrieks.

Gum points and says, "There it is!"

"There it *was*," Egg says. "I hardly saw it, and now it's gone."

"What *was* it?" Sam says.

No one has an answer for that — except Gum.

"I think we all know what it was," he says.

Egg isn't buying the escaped-alien theory, though. He raises his camera and lights up the gallery with flash photo after flash photo, but they don't see any sign of whatever it was.

His photos don't show any evidence of a creature.

"Excuse me," the sergeant says, arms crossed. "Flash photography is not permitted in this gallery."

"Oh, sorry," Egg says, clicking off the display of his camera. "I was hoping the light would show whatever just ran along the wall back there."

The sergeant looks at him with her eyebrows high. "I didn't see anything," she says.

TURN THE PAGE.

"Oh, you liar," Gum says.

"Excuse me?" the sergeant says.

"We all know what it was, too," Gum says. "It was the escaped alien."

"The what?" the sergeant says.

"Don't deny it!" Gum rants. "The alien escaped, and that's why the museum has no visitors today. But you probably forgot we had a field trip planned."

"What are you raving about? I have no idea what you mean," the sergeant says.

Gum goes on. "So we show up, and now you're trying to figure out a way to get this field trip over with before one of us sees the alien," he says. "That's probably why you and the rest of the staff seemed so nervous when we got here."

"That's the most absurd thing I've ever heard," the sergeant says.

She turns her back on Gum. "Now, if everyone will please gather at the benches and find a seat, we can start the film."

Turn to page 96.

"So many clues," Sam says, shaking her head, "and we're staying with the tour. Maybe this should be a body snatchers investigation."

"What does that mean?" Cat says.

"We're not acting like ourselves," Sam says. "Maybe some aliens switched bodies with us."

Gum's eyes go wide. "I hadn't even thought of that possibility!" he says.

"If you'll follow me," the sergeant says, leading the tour down a hallway toward a sign reading *Officers' Club*.

The kids gather outside two closed, heavy-looking wooden doors. They're marked with peeling gold lettering: *Officers Only*.

"The base officers were given some special perks," the sergeant says. "Normally, I wouldn't be allowed to let you kids in here, since you're not officers."

All together, the students say, "Awww!"

The sergeant laughs. "But maybe today we'll make an exception." She swings open the double doors.

TURN THE PAGE.

Inside, everything is dark wood and leather. There's gold trim on the furniture, heavy red curtains on the windows at the back of the large room, and fancy-looking chandeliers hanging over a huge dining table, a sitting area, and a red-felted billiards table.

"Whoa," Sam says, moving slowly into the room, overcome with awe. "This place is amazing."

She runs a hand along the billiard table's bumper and spins to face the sergeant. "Can we shoot some pool?"

Sergeant Houlihan laughs. "Oh, no," she says. "We don't even have balls and cues for it. Nowadays, we just admire how lovely . . . oh, no."

"What's wrong?" Egg says.

The sergeant leans down for a close look at the pool table. "The cloth," she says. "It's all scratched."

She shoots Sam a wicked glare. "Did you do this?" she snaps.

"What?" Sam says. "I barely touched it. Of course I didn't do it."

The sergeant doesn't seem to hear her. Instead, Sergeant Houlihan moves through the room, squinting at couch cushions and running her fingertips along the edge of ornate side tables.

By the time she's reached the other side of the officers' lounge, her face is red with anger.

Slowly, she turns and glowers at the small group of kids from science club.

"This," she says, her voice deep and terrifying, "is what comes of letting *children* roam wild around the base."

"Wait a second," Egg says. "No one's roaming wild — "

"Except for the escaped aliens!" Gum shouts, interrupting his friend.

"Where's the secret laboratory?" Sam demands, mostly because it's more fun than standing there, being berated by a cranky museum tour guide.

"There's no secret lab!" the sergeant yells, her expression strained.

"Lies!" Gum says.

TURN TO PAGE 99.

"With all of Gum's ranting today," Cat says, her arm around Egg's shoulders, "you probably just imagined something wild in the exam room."

"Ranting?" Gum rants. "Who's ranting?"

"Certainly not you," Sam says, winking at Cat.

Egg ignores his friends' hijinks. "I'm sure I saw it," he says, as the four of them hurry to catch up with the rest of the tour.

"We can't tell the sergeant," Sam says. "She doesn't like us."

"What?" Gum says. "Who wouldn't like *us*? We're the best!"

"I think Sam's right," Egg says. "She doesn't seem like the kind of grown-up who trusts kids."

"Then you'll need proof," Sam says. "No one can argue with hard, solid evidence."

"Like what?" Cat says.

Sam shrugs. They're with the group now, and the sergeant is at the head of the tour explaining something about the surgical bay under the window beside them.

"You know," Sam says. "Fingerprints. Footprints. DNA matches. Photographs. Things like that."

Egg suddenly brightens, and he snaps his fingers. "Photographs!" he says. "That's why I was in the exam room. To take photos."

"Let's see," Gum says.

Egg switches on the display of his camera and shuffles through the most recent photos.

Egg is a thorough photographer, and his storage cards can hold thousands of photos. In the exam room alone, he probably snapped almost a hundred.

"Wow," Sam says. "This could take all day."

"Oh!" Cat says suddenly, sneaking a peak between Sam's and Egg's shoulders.

"What?" Egg says. "Did you see something?"

Cat shakes her head. "I thought I did," she says. "But it doesn't make sense."

"It might," Egg says, turning toward Cat.

TURN THE PAGE.

"I just . . ." Cat says. "Nah, never mind."

"I know what she saw," Gum says, leaning on the wall beside them. "That was her cute-animal alarm."

"What?" Sam says.

"Her cute-animal alarm!" Gum says. "Whenever Cat sees a cute animal, she goes, 'Oh!'"

Cat and Egg laugh at Gum's impression of Cat.

"Maybe she's onto something," Sam says. "Scroll back a few photos. Slowly."

Egg clicks back through the photos. He and Sam peer carefully at the screen.

"Oh!" Cat says. She laughs. "There's the alarm."

"Ah!" Sam says, tapping the screen. "Right there. Cat's cute-animal alarm works like a charm!"

Sticking out from under the steel counter is a long, bushy, gray and black ringed tail.

"A raccoon!" Cat says.

"Excuse me," Sam calls over the tour group. "Sergeant Houlihan?"

TURN TO PAGE 103.

The science club members all find a spot on the benches, angled to face a dark red curtain hanging at the back of the room.

The room goes even darker as the lighted signs and exhibit spotlights are dimmed for the film.

Suddenly Sam lets out another sneeze: "Achoo!"

Everyone jumps — and the dark red curtain pulls from the wall. Something is under it.

The thing, covered by the curtain, darts toward the benches.

The kids scream and leap from their seats. Everyone runs from the room.

Egg doesn't even have a chance to get a photo before he, too, is shoved out of the gallery.

Soon, the kids are standing in the dark doorway between the gallery and the rest of the hangar.

The thing under the curtain sprints out the huge doors at the far end, dragging the fabric with it. Only when it's out in the sunshine does it shimmy from under the curtain and take off.

But by then, it's much too far away to identify.

"There it goes," Gum says. "The alien has escaped."

He glances at the sergeant. "You'd better notify the president," he says. "She'll want to know about this."

The sergeant rolls her eyes. "Franklin Middle School Science Club," she announces to the gathered, terrified students. "This marks the end of your visit to the base museum this morning."

"What?" Egg says as Ms. Marlow and a handful of other students arrive from their tour of the rec center. "But we were supposed to be here till after lunch."

"Due to unforeseen issues," the sergeant explains, "with the theater, and an inoperative emergency door, I'm calling an early end to the field trip."

She speaks more quietly to Ms. Marlow. "We'll be sure your tickets can be used again at a later date," she says, "once all this has been dealt with."

TURN THE PAGE.

As the bus rumbles along the road back toward River City, Gum glumly stares out the window.

"You all right?" Cat asks.

Gum shrugs. "I'm just imagining that alien out there," he says. "He's probably lost in the woods, terrified."

"Or she," Cat points out.

"I just wish we'd seen him," Gum says, "or her. Or it."

Cat pats his shoulder and goes back to talking to Egg and Sam across the aisle.

It might just be his imagination, but right then Gum notices something in the woods just off the road. It's small and mostly hidden in shadows, with red little eyes.

But Gum is sure it sees him too, just for that instant as the bus zooms by. He smiles to himself: he is pretty sure he just made interplanetary peace.

THE END

To follow another path, turn to page 11.

He's about to turn and face the other club members when a lamp in the corner suddenly topples, crashing to the carpet. The lightbulbs shatter, sending white glass dust in a cloud like a mini-explosion.

The sergeant screams. Cat shrieks and backs against the wall, knocking into the light switch and dropping the whole lounge into near-pitch darkness.

Everyone flees, even the sergeant. She pushes her way past the kids, muttering to herself, "What if they're right? What if it *is* aliens?"

The kids hurry after her, through the museum lobby and toward the front entrance. Ms. Marlow and her group are passing through at just the same moment.

"What is going on here?" Ms. Marlow says.

They all stand together at the front doors as Sergeant Houlihan sprints across the parking lot, climbs into her car, and speeds away.

The guard at the gate barely has time to open it before she goes barreling through.

TURN THE PAGE.

Her car vanishes on the long gravel road back to the highway in a cloud of dust.

"Wow," Gum says, his voice quiet, almost reverent. "She admitted it."

Sam's eyebrows go up. She'd heard the sergeant's terrified muttering too. "Yeah," Sam says. "She kinda did."

Ms. Marlow checks her watch and clucks her tongue. "Well, I guess the field trip is over," she says. "Let's get on the bus."

A few minutes later, the bus is rumbling along the gravel road back toward the highway. Gum sits with Cat in the last seat, across the aisle from Sam and Egg.

Gum stares glumly out the bus's back window.

"Don't feel so bad," Cat says. "We got about as close as anyone to finding the secret aliens of Zone 99 today."

"I just wish we'd gotten real proof," Gum says.

Cat nods. Then she turns back to Sam and Egg.

TURN TO PAGE 102.

Gum stares at the base as it grows smaller on the horizon. Just as it's about to vanish, a little black shape pops up from the roof.

It shimmers above the base and then zooms into the sky, vanishing into the clouds.

Eyes and mouth wide, Gum turns to Cat. "Did you see it?" he says.

Cat, still laughing at something Sam said, looks at Gum. "See what?"

"The spaceship," Gum says. "It just took off from the base."

"Spaceship?" Egg says. He looks at Sam and Cat. "Is he serious?"

"Maybe his imagination got the better of him," Sam suggests.

"I'm telling you!" Gum says. "I saw it!"

His friends shake their heads and go back to their conversation, but Gum knows what he saw. He leans back, looks out the window, and smiles.

THE END

TO FOLLOW ANOTHER PATH, TURN TO PAGE 11.

"Yes, what is it?" the sergeant says, obviously annoyed at being interrupted during the tour.

"My friend Edward was in the exam room after the tour left," Sam says.

"That's not allowed!" the sergeant says.

"I know that," Egg says, "and I'm sorry, but you have to see the photo I took."

The sergeant waits a beat, and then waves Egg to the front of the group.

He holds out the display to Sergeant Houlihan and points at the tail.

"What *is* that?" the sergeant says.

"A raccoon tail!" Cat calls from the back of the group.

The sergeant squints at Cat. A moment later, the sergeant's eyes go wide as she begins to see what the sleuths have discovered.

"This is back in the exam room?" Sergeant Houlihan asks.

TURN THE PAGE.

The four friends nod.

"Just a couple of minutes ago," Egg confirms.

The sergeant pulls the walkie-talkie from her hip, clicks the button, and says, "Anyone from maintenance, we got a trash panda in the med wing, over."

She releases the button and waits.

Cat frowns. "Trash panda," she mutters to her friends. "What a mean thing to say. Though pandas are cute, and raccoons *do* eat trash. Still, it sounds so mean."

The walkie-talkie crackles. "Roger that, Sarge. Up in a tick."

When maintenance arrives with a couple of county employees in tan uniforms, the field trip friends gather just outside the exam room door.

After some quick searching, they find the raccoon hidden in a vent behind the counter.

The man from maintenance unscrews the access panel and backs away quickly.

A county employees catches it with a cinching lasso. She pulls out a fat raccoon, its little hands still clutching a plastic wrapper.

"She's a big one!" says the woman from the county. "And she's been snacking!"

Sure enough, the raccoon's face is dusted with what looks like powdered sugar.

The sergeant says, "Looks like she got into the box lunches we had for the kids."

The man from maintenance nods. "That's a powdered doughnut face, for sure," he says.

"Oh, man!" Gum says, forlorn. "We were going to have powdered doughnuts?"

Egg pats Gum on the back. "Don't feel too bad," he says. "At least we caught the alien!"

"Oh, ha ha," Gum says. "You're so funny."

But Sam, Egg, and Cat hardly hear him over their own laughter.

THE END

TO FOLLOW ANOTHER PATH, TURN TO PAGE 11.

literary news

MYSTERIOUS WRITER REVEALED!

Steve Brezenoff is the author of the Field Trip Mysteries, the Museum Mysteries, and the Ravens Pass series of thrillers, as well as three novels for older readers. Steve lives in Minneapolis, Minnesota, with his wife, Beth, and their two children, Sam and Etta.

arts & entertainment

ARTIST IS KEY TO SOLVING MYSTERY, SAY POLICE

Marcos Calo lives happily in A Coruña, Spain, with his wife, Patricia (who is also an illustrator), and their daughter, Claudia. When Marcos and Patricia aren't drawing, they like to go on long walks by the sea. They also watch a lot of films and eat Nutella sandwiches. Yum!

A Detective's Dictionary

barracks – a building or area that houses soldiers

berated – to criticize someone or to yell at them

delusional – to believe something that is obviously untrue

hangar – the place where aircraft are kept

hankering – a desire for something

labyrinth – a maze or a place with a lot of confusing paths

mischievous – willing to cause playful trouble

mortified – feeling embarrassed

otoscope – a medical instrument to examine inner ears

reverent – being very respectful

skulk – to move around in a secretive way

translucent – something that is not transparent, but allows light to shine through

FURTHER INVESTIGATIONS
CASE #YCSFTMTOFOSSI7

1. Gum believes that aliens exist and that the Air Force base is hiding them. Is there anything in the text that would make you think that is true as well? Is there anything that would make you think it's not true?

2. In one of the paths, the four sleuths all admit they wished they had seen aliens. Why do you think that is? Would you want to see aliens?

3. Cat and Egg like to go tell adults when something is suspicious. Gum and Sam like to investigate. Which do you like to do: tell an adult or investigate? Why?

IN YOUR OWN DETECTIVE'S NOTEBOOK . . .

1. Pretend you're Gum writing a letter to the Air Force base before the field trip. What would you write? What questions would you ask?

2. Ms. Marlow assigns the field trip students a paper after the trip. Choosing one of the field trip mystery kids — Egg, Sam, Gum, or Cat — write about your experience in the base.

3. What field trips do you want to go on? Write five places you would love to visit with your class and explain the reasons why.

Ready to choose your next MYSTERY?

Check out all the books in the You Choose Stories Field Trip Mysteries!